DOGFISH
Just be YOU!
WRITTEN BY Rita Reed
ILLUSTRATED BY Craig Cartwright

Dogfish, Just be YOU!
Published by Fine Eye Media
Thousand Oaks, CA

Publisher's Cataloging-in-Publication data
Names: Reed, Rita, author. | Cartwright, Craig, illustrator.
Title: Dogfish, just Be YOU! / Rita Reed ; illustrations by Craig Cartwright.
Description: Thousand Oaks, CA : Fine Eye Media, [2023] | Series: Dogfish tales. | Audience: Juvenile. | Summary: Dogfish is unique and special in his own way, but often doubts himself. In this Arctic adventure, Dogfish admires his friend's abilities and wishes he could be like them. But when disaster strikes, will Dogfish believe in himself enough to save the day? A story about believing in yourself and that everyone is perfect and special in their own way!--Publisher.
Identifiers: ISBN: 978-1-7357862-4-7 (paperback) | 978-1-7357862-5-4 (hardcover)
Subjects: LCSH: Dogfish--Juvenile fiction. | Whales--Juvenile fiction. | Self-acceptance--Juvenile fiction. | Self-esteem--Juvenile fiction. | Self-confidence--Juvenile fiction. | Arctic regions--Juvenile fiction. | Auroras--Juvenile fiction. | Ocean--Juvenile fiction. | CYAC: Dogfish--Fiction. | Whales--Fiction. | Self-acceptance--Fiction. | Self-esteem--Fiction. | Self-confidence--Fiction. | Arctic regions--Fiction. | Auroras--Fiction. | Ocean--Fiction. | BISAC: JUVENILE FICTION / Social Themes / Self-Esteem & Self-Reliance.
Classification: LCC: PZ7.1.R431 D64 2023 | DDC: [Fic]--dc23

Cover and Interior design by Victoria Wolf, wolfdesignandmarketing.com. Copyright owned by Rita Reed.

Illustrations by Craig Cartwright.

FINEEYEMEDIA

To all the children—

Everyone is special in their own way, and you are PERFECT just the way you are!

My son Aaron, wrote the following words of love and encouragement to his sister upon her college graduation:

"Never doubt yourself and KEEP MOVING FORWARD, you have so much to offer the world!"

— Aaron Gottlieb 1994–2020

A booming band of whales sang as Dogfish jumped out of bed, with dreams of the northern lights still floating through his head.

His ears wiggled and twitched
as he happily traveled along,
following the humpback whales
as they sang their whaley songs.

The pod gleefully welcomed him and extended an invitation, "Dogfish will you join us on our northern migration?"

Dogfish happily accepted and politely requested, "Will we see the AURORA BOREALIS?

Since I was a pup, it's been a dream of mine to see the colorful lights dancing in the sky!"

The humpbacks
winked and said,
"Possibly."

Happy and carefree, the whales breached.
Twisting and leaping out of the sea,
landing with a crash and a huge

SPLASH!

Dogfish was amazed that they were so graceful, with their ENORMOUS size and gigantic tails!

Dogfish wished HE was a humpback whale!

A little voice inside his head swirled,
"Never doubt yourself and
KEEP MOVING FORWARD.
You have so much to
offer the world!"

Then out of the dark,
flashes of black and white
dashed and circled,
giving them all a fright!

The orcas played ball as they all headed north,
tossing it effortlessly back and forth.

Dogfish was astonished at how they
threw the ball. They were so athletic!
(He didn't play sports at all.)

Dogfish
wished
HE was an
orca!

Again, the voice inside his head swirled,
"Never doubt yourself and
KEEP MOVING FORWARD.
You have so much to
offer the world!"

They swam past Alaska and the Bering Sea.
The waters were cold and very icy!

As they entered the Arctic, they
heard lovely sounds. A band of belugas
with heads big and round!

Their singing was exquisite, such a
beautiful sound. Dogfish couldn't sing—
He just barked and howled!

Dogfish wished
HE was a beluga!

Reminding himself again,
"Never doubt yourself and
KEEP MOVING FORWARD.
You have so much to
offer the world!"

Smiley, silly narwhals swam into sight. Happy and hilarious they played with delight.

Dogfish admired their shiny, ivory horns. Mystical and magical, the ocean's UNICORNS!

Dogfish wished
HE was a narwhal!

Whaley songs grew louder in the icy cold sea. The crowd swam faster, picking up their speed.

Dogfish was tired and
feeling a little blue,
thinking of all the things
that he just couldn't do.

"I can try to be like a humpback
or the unicorns of the sea.
I could be like a beluga . . . but why?
I am the BEST ME I can be!"

Suddenly . . .

His big fluffy ears wiggled and rotated. With his SUPER SONIC HEARING, distress signals were located!

Dogfish rushed to the commotion.
Baby polar bear was ALONE in the ocean!

"I was playing when the ice broke;
now I'm floating out to sea.
Help me PLEASE!"

Then without any doubt,

Dogfish kept MOVING FORWARD

He pushed that huge iceberg

all the way back to shore!

A dream came true
for that pup as he
looked up ...

Shining bright, dancing in the sky,

glowing and glistening, the NORTHERN LIGHTS!

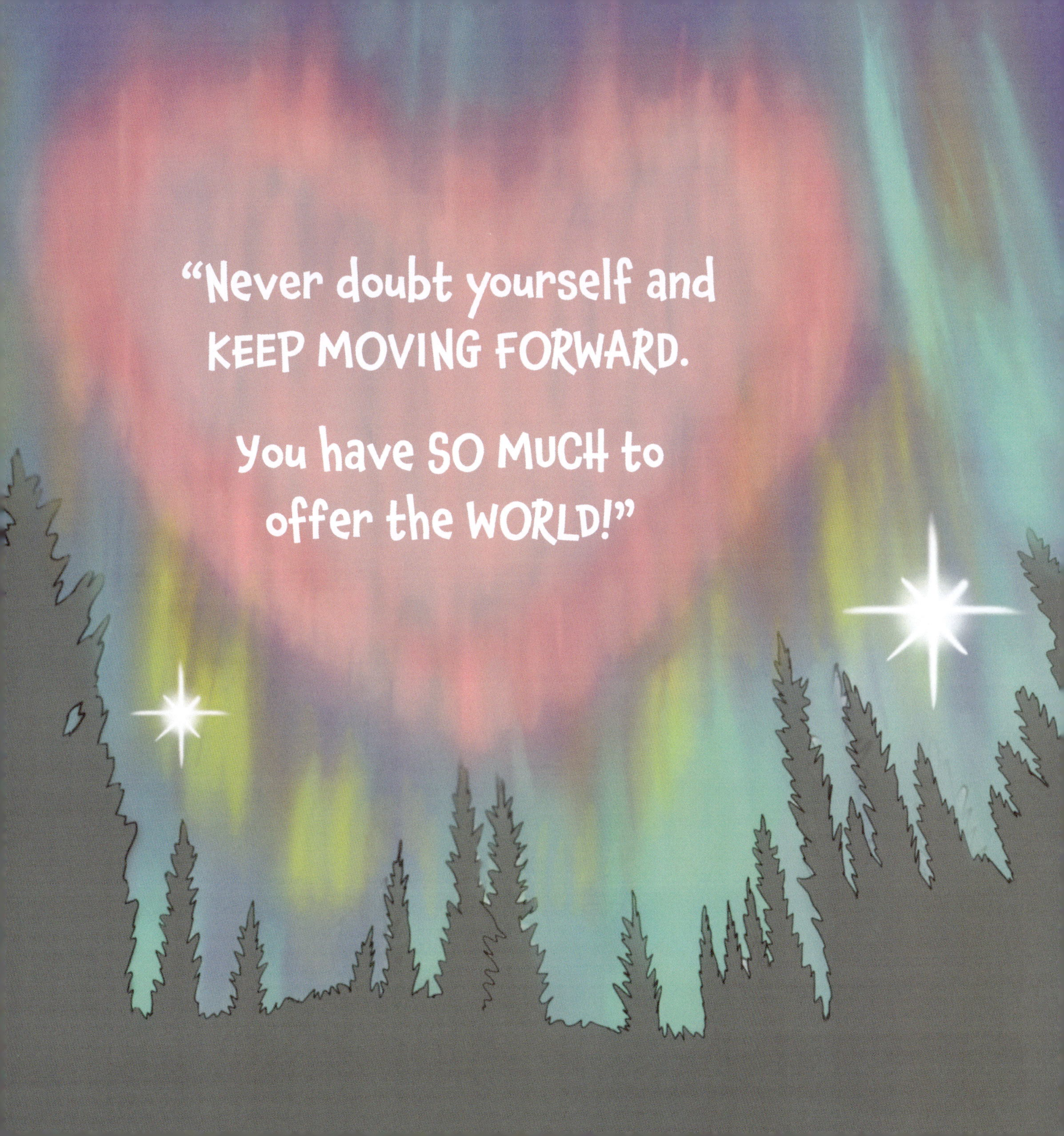

"Never doubt yourself and KEEP MOVING FORWARD.

You have SO MUCH to offer the WORLD!"

Arctic Ocean
Bering Sea
United States Of America (Alaska)
Canada
North Pacific Ocean
Santa Monica Bay
United States Of America

About the Author

Rita Reed lives in Southern California, where she studied art, interior design, and architecture. She enjoys spending time with her family and two silly, spoiled cats.

Rita has found extraordinary joy in creating the magical Dogfish Tales series. Through these books, she hopes to spread love, inclusiveness, positivity, and acceptance of all.

"I feel Dogfish in my heart. He's the vulnerable, innocent child in all of us."

About the Illustrator

Craig Cartwright has worked in all aspects of the visual arts world including children's books, editorial illustration, character design, and film and commercial storyboards.

His client list includes Pixar, Disney, Warner Brother (Looney Tunes), Fox (The Simpsons), The History Channel, The Family Guy, and Marvel.

Craig received a degree in commercial illustration from Commonwealth University in Virginia. He lives in Venice, California.

More Books in the Dogfish Tales Series

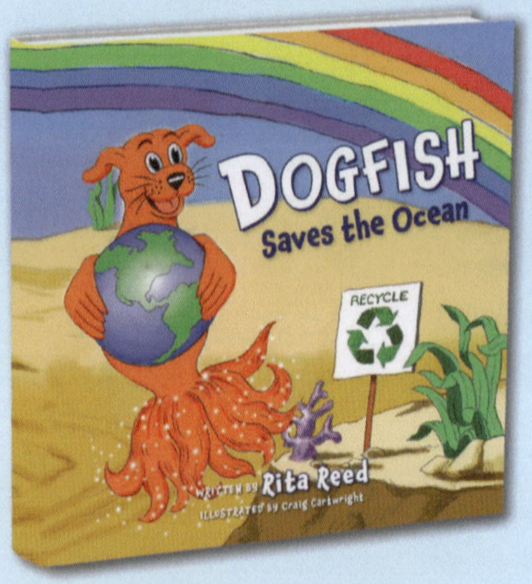

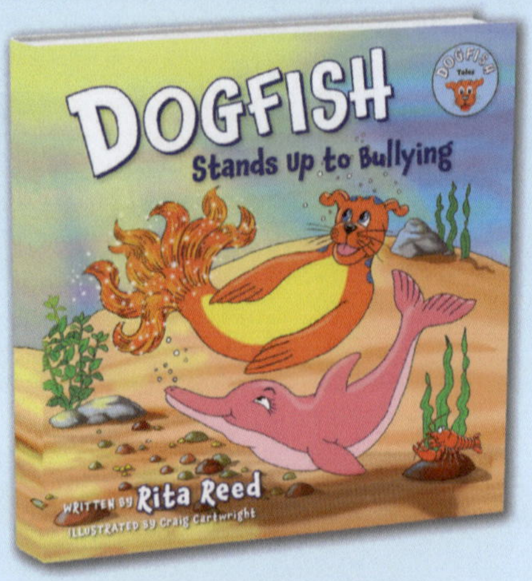

Follow Rita and the Dogfish Tales Series:

dogfishtales.com | @dogfishtales @_rita_reed_

Printed in Great Britain
by Amazon

20409122R00022